THE BEACH COLLECTOR

THE FIRST STORIES

ABOUT THE AUTHOR

Originally from the Caribbean islands of Trinidad and Martinique, Antonia is a writer of poetry and prose. She has travelled extensively. All through her childhood and on her travels, she has collected and bottled sand, coral, shells and driftwood off beaches from Hawaii to the Red Sea, the Caribbean to the shores of Ireland. She has put her adult writing on hold to spend time writing stories for her grandchildren and regaling them with beach tales capturing the magic of her travels and the shores she has visited.

THE BEACH COLLECTOR

COLLECTOR

THE FIRST STORIES

Antonia 'GranT' Smith

Matador
9 Priory Business Park,
Wistow Road, Kibworth Beauchamp,
Leicestershire. LE8 0RX
Tel: 0116 279 2299
Email: books@troubador.co.uk
Web: www.troubador.co.uk/matador
Twitter: @matadorbooks

ISBN 978 1789015 041

British Library Cataloguing in Publication Data.
A catalogue record for this book is available from the British Library.

Printed and bound in the UK by TJ International, Padstow, Cornwall
Typeset in 11pt Minion Pro by Troubador Publishing Ltd, Leicester, UK

Matador is an imprint of Troubador Publishing Ltd

for Aitana
Read and enjoy
GranT

*I dedicate this first collection of beach stories to my darling
grandchildren: Elise, Coco, Nia, Louis, Idaisa (Didi) and
Joseph – thank you for listening to my stories and inspiring
me to write more.*

Your GranT

*In memory of Patricia Worrell,
This book is yours too. RIP 2018*

IMPORTANT NOTE TO THE READER:

Although the stories are numbered, they do not follow on one from the other. These are Grandma's memories, and they skip backwards and forwards in time.

THE FIRST BEACH ADVENTURE

Coco was four years old. She loved going to visit her grandma. Her grandma collected beaches, made of real sand and sea shells and pebbles of different colours and shapes. She kept them in plates or bottles laid on their sides. She let Coco play with the beaches and run the sand through her fingers while she told her about the beach where she had picked up the sand and the shells. Well, nearly all the beaches… There were a few beaches that Grandma never opened or uncovered.

One day Coco's little brother Louis lifted off the heavy glass bell cover over one of Grandma's special beaches. The little girl had never touched Grandma's special beaches because she was too well-behaved and knew she should ask first. But her brother Louis did not ask first. He just went ahead and lifted the cover off.

Suddenly there was a 'pop' and he disappeared. Little

Coco nearly jumped out of her skin. Her eyes were as large as saucers and her mouth was wide open, but no sound was coming out of it! Her legs would not move. She just stared at the space where Louis had been.

She blinked twice and suddenly her voice came back in a loud squeak. "Mummy!" she squealed, happy that her legs were working again too. She ran off in the direction of the kitchen to find her mummy, who was having a cup of tea with her grandma.

"Mummy! Grandma! He went pop! He's gone! I can't see my little brother any more!"

"Calm down, darling," was all her mother said. "Calm down and tell us what happened."

Grown-ups are a bit slow sometimes, Coco said to herself in her head. Then she told them again: "He went pop! He's gone! I can't see Louis any more!"

Grandma turned a funny colour (a bit yellow) and got up from her chair very quickly. Mum was still saying, "Calm down," when she saw her mother dash out of the kitchen holding Coco's hand and pulling her along with her.

Grandma was saying, "Oh dear! Oh dear!" She looked at Coco and said, "Show me where you were." Coco took her to the shelf where the beach with the glass bell cover always sat. She could see that the cover was off. She looked at Coco for a minute and then said, "Close your eyes!" Coco did as she was told because we must always do what our grandma or mummy says. Coco felt a bit funny and then she heard her grandma say, "You can open them now!"

When Coco opened her eyes, there was her little brother Louis running down a lovely sandy beach, holding hands with a monkey with a long tail. He was laughing and squealing happily.

Coco couldn't help it. She let go of Grandma's hand and ran off after Louis, laughing and squealing too. Grandma shook her head and then sat down on the sand.

Louis, the monkey and Coco (who could run very fast and had caught up with her little brother in no time flat) ran into the trees. There were lots of coconut trees. Suddenly the monkey ran up one of the coconut trees and the two children stood at the bottom, looking up in amazement. "I wish we could run up a tree like that," said Coco. Suddenly she realised that she was doing it, running up the coconut tree just as the monkey had done.

At the top of the tree the monkey handed them each a whole coconut. Luckily they had magically shrunk so they were the right size for little hands. The monkey took a coconut for himself and tipped back his head, holding the coconut to his mouth. He made loud slurping noises as he drank the delicious, sweet juice.

Coco and Louis did the same and soon all three were making slurpy noises as they drank. Coco stopped first and she said politely to the monkey, "Please may I take a coconut to my grandma? I'm sure she must be very thirsty too."

The monkey nodded and handed her one. There was a slight 'pop' and they found themselves at the bottom of the tree. The monkey had disappeared.

"Let's find Grandma," said Coco as she took Louis'

hand and led him back to the beach. They walked back the way they had come and they could see Grandma sitting on the sand a little way off. They made their way to her, holding the coconut carefully.

"Did you bring me a coconut to drink? Thank you Coco, thank you Louis," said Grandma. She waited a minute for the coconut to get as big as her hand and then drank the coconut water without making a single slurpy noise. She looked very happy. "That's the best coconut I have ever tasted, my darlings. Shall we go home now?" She gently put the empty coconut down on the sand and a little wave came right up and took it away into the sea.

They could see it bobbing away on the water and getting smaller and smaller.

Grandma held out both hands at her sides and Coco and Louis put their hands in hers, but she did not move. The children looked up at her, wondering how they were going to get back home. She looked at each of them in turn and said softly, "You have discovered my magic beach, and now all my beaches are magic, but you must not tell anyone about it, not even your mama or daddy. OK?"

Coco nodded her head solemnly and so did Louis, but he didn't really understand.

"One day I will tell you all about it, I promise," continued Grandma.

"Please may we come back here again, Grandma?" asked Coco, eyes shining with excitement.

"Yes, I suppose we can. But there are lots of other places I want to show you too." Grandma smiled her special smile, then holding their hands tightly, she said suddenly,

"Now jump!" Louis had no trouble understanding what that meant and both children jumped a giant jump and landed laughing in Grandma's sitting room, just as their mummy came through the doorway saying, "There you are Louis. See Coco, he hasn't disappeared at all."

Coco looked at her grandma and laughed, and laughed.

THE SPECIAL BEACH AND THE PETRIFIED FOREST

It was Saturday and that meant the day of Elise's birthday party had come at last. On Wednesday she became six. She was very excited because her mummy had invited some of her friends to come and play. She had never really had a party with school friends before. She couldn't wait to show them all the tricks she could do on the swings at the bottom of the garden.

Best of all though was the surprise that Mummy had planned with her Taty Zou.

The children called their aunts 'Taty' if they spoke French and 'Aunty' if they spoke English. It was a habit they had picked up from their French cousins in Martinique. In Trinidad and Tobago, where Grandma and Grandpa and their three daughters were born, it was the custom for children to call their parents' adult friends 'Aunty'.

Her cousin and best friend, Coco, was coming to play as well. Even better was the fact that she was coming for a sleepover! But Elise didn't know that.

That morning, when she visited her Grandma's room with her little sister, Elise had been given some nice new clothes wrapped in pretty paper with lots of cupcakes on it and a lovely card. Then they all trooped downstairs. Instead of dashing off to work as usual, Grandma made scrambled eggs, toasted bagels and sausages for breakfast. She even made braids in Elise's hair with beads at the ends. Elise was very happy.

Grandpa was busy outside with the gardener, Paul, getting the garden ready for Elise and her friends. Poor Elise felt she could burst with excitement. Little did she know that it was going to be a very surprising birthday indeed.

It was a lovely, sunny day. Her friends came and they played out in the garden for an hour. Then they came in for snacks and pizza and pasta with pesto (Elise's favourite). They had her favourite juice drinks – the ones that came in little coloured bottles. Coco arrived in the midst of it all and she hugged Elise and wished her a happy birthday. Coco's little brother Louis also wished Elise a happy birthday and her Taty Zou gave her a lovely hug. Everybody gave her presents.

When everyone left at the end of the day, Elise felt quite tired. She had done lots of swinging and showed everyone her tricks on the swings and the trapeze. Mummy was just saying something to Taty Zou about the cake, but she wasn't sure. She wondered if she could eat any more… She flopped down on the sofa and Coco came and sat next to her. They held hands and talked about stuff.

"Grandma!" shouted little Nia and Louis when their grandma came through the door and into the kitchen. She was smiling as usual and gave her grandchildren big hugs in turns. Then she took off her coat and came to sit down in the living room where Elise and Coco were talking.

"There's something I want to show you Elise," Grandma said, winking at Coco. "Coco, shall we show Elise our little secret?"

Elise's mummy came in just then to say that she was going upstairs to change baby Joe's nappy and clothes because he had done a big poo.

Elise and Coco laughed and wrinkled up their noses saying, "Poo! Yucky!!" Of course Nia and Louis also wrinkled up their noses and said, "Poo! Yucky!"

Elise's mummy went off up the stairs with baby Joe. The girls couldn't stop giggling for ages. Grandma waited patiently until they calmed down.

Little Nia, who was three, looked up at Grandma and asked, "Can I see the secret too, Grandma?"

"Of course you may, darling," said Grandma with a smile.

Elise had started to jump around in excitement and Nia decided to jump around too.

"Hold hands," said Grandma, standing up.

They all held hands and Grandma went over to her special beach (the one with the heavy glass cover).

"Can I take the cover off, Grandma?" asked Coco eagerly. Grandma nodded and Coco carefully lifted the heavy glass cover off and rested it down on the shelf next to the beach.

In case you didn't know, Grandma collected beaches. They were made up of sand and whatever else she found on the beaches she visited – shells, pebbles, even seaweed!

"Hold hands," Grandma said firmly, and with her one free hand, she touched her special shell.

All Elise and Nia heard was the 'pop' before they found themselves on the longest, most beautiful beach they had ever seen.

Waves were rolling in gently and frothing on the warm, wet sand. "Hmmm," said Grandma, "it looks like the tide is coming in. So, children," she said, looking around at each of the four in turn, "you may go into the water, but not too far."

"But Grandma," the two bigger girls started to speak at the same time, "we can't go into the water with all our clothes on!"

Little Nia gave a raucous laugh like a crow and looked down at her tummy. "Waah!" they all exclaimed together. "We have our swimming costumes on!"

In they went and started frolicking in the warm water, squealing with delight. They remembered what they had learnt in swimming class and somehow did not even notice that they weren't wearing their armbands. They floated and paddled and swam around. Then they heard Grandma calling.

"Come now children. I have something to show you."

Being well-behaved children they immediately called back, "Coming, Grandma!" and headed out of the water.

"This is Sainte-Anne, children, on the island of Martinique. It is another one of Grandma's favourite beaches. But come, what I want to show you is not here," said Grandma mysteriously.

"Please can we pick up some sand and shells first Grandma?" asked Coco.

Grandma smiled. "Of course," she said, "but don't be long."

They started looking for interesting shells and pebbles, bits of coral and driftwood, even little strands of seaweed. There weren't many, just lots and lots of golden sand. It looked like some giant had spilled a rather large bag of breadcrumbs all along the edge of the water. They each managed a small pile and Grandma showed them a place at the end of the beach where they could leave their treasure to dry out a bit on the rocks.

Then she said, "Hold hands and close your eyes," and when they did they heard a little 'pop' and then they found themselves in the strangest place.

"This is the petrified forest," explained Grandma. "Everything here has been turned into stone." The children couldn't believe their eyes as they picked up what looked like shells, bits of wood, leaves, and smooth bits of glass. They blinked and screwed up their eyes because although those things looked like shells, wood, leaves and glass, they all felt like stones!

"How did this happen, Grandma?" asked Coco in a voice full of wonder, but with a little bit of fear mixed in.

Then she asked the question they were all afraid to ask. "Will we turn into stone as well, Grandma?"

Grandma smiled her gentle smile. "No, you won't turn into stone because you would have to stand very still in one place, for a very long time. It has taken hundreds of years for the salty wind from the sea, the hot sun and the dry, dry air to turn all these things into stone! This is a very special place," she said, "there are only one or two places in all the world where this has happened."

"Can we go home now?" whispered Elise. She liked to jump around all the time and she really didn't want to be turned into stone.

"Hold hands and close your eyes then, children," said Grandma.

One small 'pop' later, they were all back in the living room and their mummies were just coming in through the door.

"Remember," whispered Grandma, "this is our secret."

"We forgot the sand and shells!" exclaimed Nia.

"Sh-h-h!" said everybody else, except for the mummies, who looked around and asked, "What's the big secret then?"

The children looked at Grandma and started to giggle helplessly.

THE STRANGE BEACH AT LA ROMAINE-ON-SEA

"Ai-ee-ee-ee!" Coco suddenly found herself screaming at the top of her lungs as she clung to the liana for her life! Below her the cliff dropped off, not too steeply, but it was a clear run to the muddy 'beach' at the bottom.

"Whee-ee!" she heard another voice just next to her, squealing in excitement and pleasure. She turned her head to look as the liana swung back towards the cliff. She looked up and she could see the roots of the tree as it clung to a thin ledge of earth above her. Luckily she did not swing all the way back. She breathed a loud sigh of relief as she realised that she would not be crashing into the face of the cliff.

She turned to look again and watched in awe and puzzlement as the skinny, lanky girl let go of her liana and tumbled down the slope. Who was she? Why did she look so familiar? And where was Grandma?? Would she be coming soon to help her get down? Coco wondered.

Her liana swung more and more slowly as she watched the girl making her way back up the slope, clutching at reeds and grasses as she climbed. As she got closer and closer, Coco thought that she really did look very familiar. *I know,* thought Coco, *she looks a bit like my Taty Tsui!* Surely it couldn't be her?

"Jump!" called the girl. "It's fun! I won't let you slide all the way down. Jump to me!"

Coco was not convinced, but something in the girl's voice made her feel safe and besides, she couldn't very well hang there forever... so she closed her eyes and let go, willing herself to land close to her new friend. She was surprised to find that she floated down gently and landed just at the girl's feet. She was laughing as Coco opened her eyes, and then opened them even wider because she recognised that face now – it was her grandma's face.

"Grandma, is it really you?" gasped Coco. "Is that really, really you?"

"Yes darling, it is. This place is where I grew up and this is where I used to play cowboys and cowgirls when I was little. This is the only place where I can be a child again. Come, I'll take you down to the shore."

They made their way down the hill and Coco was glad that her brother Louis hadn't come along on this adventure. He would have been very, very scared. But it would have been so nice to have someone her own age to share the adventure with.

"Grandma?" she asked slowly.

"Yes?" replied Grandma, cocking one eyebrow.

"Next time, could we bring Elise on our adventure? And Louis, and Nia and Didi and little Joe too?"

"Sure, darling, we'll bring them all along the next time. Now we should take our shoes off and leave them where it's dry."

"Ooh! My feet are sinking, Grandma!" cried Coco. "It feels like mud!"

"That's because it *is* mud, sweetheart."

"Where did the sand go?" asked Coco.

"Do you see that little island out there in the sea?" Grandma pointed a little to the right. "The one with the house on it? Well, that's where the sand is, I think. That's where the sea began years and years ago. Every year it has crept further and further in, eating up the land like a greedy monster."

"I didn't know the sea could eat the land like that!" Coco was surprised. "Is that why there aren't any shells here?" Then she suddenly had a thought. "Will the sea eat us up as well?"

"No darling," replied Grandma with a gentle smile, "we would have to stay very still for years and years at the edge of the water, and we aren't going to do that, are we?"

Coco shook her head. Then she said, "The water is very warm, Grandma. It really feels quite funny to wiggle my toes in the mud. Did you do that when you were a little girl?"

"I used to come down here with my dogs and we would play in the water," Grandma said, with a faraway

14

look in her eyes. "They loved to have a swim. It does feel quite funny to wiggle our toes in the mud, doesn't it? Shall we go for a little walk along my beach?"

Holding hands with the young Grandma, Coco looked left and right. "Let's go this way Grandma," she said. "I would like to see those coconut trees over there."

"Who knows?" said Grandma. "Perhaps we will find a baby coconut tree, or some other interesting thing."

"Grandma, how could you make a beach when there's only mud here?" Coco was very perplexed about this question.

"If we look really hard, we might find something beachy, but you know, Coco, there isn't always sand where the sea meets the land. Can you guess what other things there might be?"

"I know. Rocks!" said Coco. She loved guessing games.

"That's right," said Grandma, "rocks! Can you think of anything else?"

"Yes," said Coco with a smile, "mud!!"

They walked along for a little while and Coco was really excited when they reached the coconut trees, because there at the edge of the water was a coconut with a baby coconut tree growing out of it. There were other dark, round things near to the baby coconut tree. They looked like hard little balls.

"When I was a little girl, we used to play cricket with those. We would use an old coconut branch for a bat," said Grandma, in a soft voice with that faraway look in her eyes again. "These come from Venezuela, over there." Grandma was pointing out to sea.

"How do you know they are from Vene... Vene...?" Coco was having trouble getting the word right.

"Venezuela, darling." Then Grandma explained, "I know that because there aren't any of those trees here. Look at the water, Coco, do you see that big yellow streak? That's river water that has come all the way from Venezuela. It's a current and it brings all sorts of things across the Gulf... even people sometimes."

Coco wondered whether Grandma was pulling her leg. Then she remembered that Grandma was a real stickler for the truth, so what she said must be true! But a river in the sea? That did sound rather strange.

"We should go back now," said Grandma, and Coco thought she sounded a little sad.

"It was fun seeing you as a little girl, Grandma. We must come here again with all my cousins and my little brother." Coco took Grandma's outstretched hand and together they closed their eyes and jumped...

4

A QUICK 'VENTURE TO THE PINK SAND

"Why do you collect beaches, Grandma?" asked Nia with her very serious face on.

"I have always collected shells," said Grandma. "When I was a little girl I used to make jewellery as presents for my mummy and daddy. I didn't collect sand because I lived on an island with sandy beaches all around. But when I went away to university I missed the feel of sand running through my fingers and I missed all my beautiful shells. So, one day when I was sitting in the sand on my favourite beach – Mayaro, in Trinidad – I picked up a handful of sand and put it in my pocket, and I picked up a piece of driftwood and those seed pods we call sea eggs – the ones that float in from far away – and one of those hard fruits that we used to play cricket on the beach…"

"Was that your first beach?" asked Nia.

"I guess it was," said Grandma. "Then I didn't make one for years, until I went to Hawaii. That's where I got my oyster shell with the pearl inside, and the strange little bottle."

"That one is your magic beach, isn't it?" asked Nia, although she already knew the answer.

"Yes, poppet, that's right. After Hawaii I started collecting beaches every time I went to the seaside. I even had one with sea water in!"

"Why did you put them all into the big beach, Grandma?" asked Nia.

"Well, I had collected so many different beaches in bottles that there was no more space for me to lay them down. I found that big vase that your Taty Zou had left at my house, so I started putting my beaches into it and I thought it looked so beautiful. Do you see all the different colours of the sand? Isn't that amazing? There is grey and pink and black and... sandy-coloured sand." Grandma suddenly laughed. "There is not only a range of different coloured sand, but they feel different too. Some sand is silky smooth, others are gritty and pebbly. Yet others, like my Mayaro sand, are made up of crushed sea shells and coral..."

"What's coral?" asked Nia.

"Coral is alive. Well at least it starts out as a living creature, called a polyp. There are many different kinds of coral: some look like plants, some look like pretty, coloured specks. The thing is that coral polyps are really, really tiny and when they die, their bodies pile up and then stick together. That's how coral reefs are formed. Fish love to swim around the reefs and play in all the nooks and crannies."

Grandma sat down in her favourite chair and Nia climbed onto her lap. Nia loved to sit on Grandma's lap and chat.

"Where is your sister?" Grandma asked.

"She's playing with Coco upstairs in our room," said Nia.

"And Louis?"

"He only wants to play with Joe and his mummy."

"And Nia?"

"I'm here with you, Grandma! I'm right here sitting in your lap!"

"Oh yes, that's true!" said Grandma and Nia laughed out loud. Grandma loved to tease.

"Shall we have a little 'venture, just the two of us then?" Grandma asked Nia.

"Yes! Yes! I want to have a 'venture with you, Grandma."

It was only a few minutes later that Nia found herself holding Grandma's hand and standing on a long, beautiful beach with green water lapping at the sandy shore. She blinked a few times – the sand was pink!

"Look Grandma," said Nia excitedly, "the sand is pink!"

"We are in Barbados, poppet," replied Grandma, "and it's the coral that has made this sand pink. I thought I would bring you here because we were talking about corals, weren't we?"

"'Bados?" repeated Nia, missing out the first part of the word as she tended to do when she was excited. She used to talk like that all the time when she was very little, but lately she only did it when she was excited about something. "But why is the water green, Grandma?"

"Ah yes, the green water! That's because of the kind of rocks that this island is made of. It's called limestone and when it reflects the sun's rays through the water, it makes the water look green."

Grandma suddenly stopped talking and sat down on the sand. She had gone a little green herself. Nia put her hand on her grandma's cheek. "Grandma?" she said. "Shall I get you some water to drink?" She asked this but there was nowhere she could see where she could get a glass or some water to drink. She ran to the sea and came back and put two wet little hands on Grandma's forehead.

"Ahh!" sighed Grandma. "That feels good." Nia suddenly remembered something and started digging in the sand. Soon enough she came to the wet sand that felt very cool in the midday sun.

"Here Grandma, put some of this wet sand on your forehead. It will make you feel better," and it did.

A young man had been noticing what was going on and came over to them.

"My grandma needs some water to drink," said Nia.

"We can do better than that!" the young man said and then he sprinted up the beach to a spot where there were coconut trees. He quickly climbed a tree and came back down just as quickly with a smallish green coconut. He walked over to a cart that was parked on the side of the road that bordered the beach. Reaching in, he produced a large machete and cut open the coconut. He brought the coconut over to where Nia was sitting next to her grandma. Grandma accepted the coconut gratefully.

"Thank you, young man," she said, before she put it to her lips and drank deeply from the coconut. "You have some too, poppet. The sun is very hot and we should have been more careful."

Nia was very thirsty and very happily took a big drink from Grandma's coconut. It was delicious and so refreshing. "Do you want to go home now, Grandma?" asked Nia.

"Yes, poppet. Let's take Grandma home."

Grandma smiled brightly at the young man as she stood up, looking like her normal self again. "Thank you and goodbye."

"Goodbye," he answered and he headed back up the beach. When he got back to his cart he looked back, but they were gone.

"Grandma is feeling a little tired, children," Grandma was telling her grandchildren when they all wandered into the sitting room and found her sitting back in the big lounge chair with her feet up. "Maybe we could watch some cartoons on the television?"

Nia looked at Grandma and they shared a little secret smile.

THE BEACH WITH THE
HOT BLACK SAND

It was bedtime and all the children were ready for their bedtime story, dressed in pyjamas, but not really sleepy. They were having a sleepover at Grandma's house and they were excited at spending a night together. Besides this was the first time baby Joe was big enough to really hang out with the big children (his two sisters and two cousins). He had just turned two and he wanted to be around his big cousin Louis.

Louis used to call himself Lou-li when he was little. Now he was four and he could say Louis. He didn't really mind having his little cousin around, but only if he could also be with his big cousin Elise (who was seven!). Elise was always with his big sister Coco – they were best friends and cousins. His big sister was always nice to him and he was fascinated by his cousin Elise. He liked the sound of her name and he liked how she always ran around non-stop. He liked his cousin Nia too. She was only one year older than him and they were good friends.

Grandma had moved to a really fun house. There was a big room where they would all sleep together when they went to visit. Sometimes that meant that nobody got much sleep, but they did have a lot of fun playing together… and of course there were the adventures. It was hard not being able to tell their other friends about their 'ventures' but at least they could talk about them when they all got together. Where would they be going this time?

They could hear Grandma coming up the stairs. She wore a lot of bracelets so, if they were quiet, they could always tell when she was coming. Elise squealed and that set them all off.

The door opened and Grandma came in. "Why are you all awake, children?" she asked in a pretend shocked voice. They all knew she was pretending because there was a twinkle in her eye and a smile not far off.

"Grandma!" they all shouted in unison.

"Shhh!" she said. "We don't want your mummies to come in, do we? So let's whisper."

"Are we going on a 'venture, Grandma?" asked Coco in a whisper.

"Would you like to?" asked Grandma. "Aren't you tired and sleepy?"

"We're not sleepy, Grandma. Please take us on a 'venture," pleaded Coco.

"Yes. Please, Grandma, pleea-se!" they all said together.

Grandma had been standing just inside the door and she had one hand in her pocket. She came right in and took her hand out of her pocket. She opened her hand and they could all see that she had some sand in her hand and the magic shell.

"I'll take you to the beach where the sand is black," she said in her quiet voice. "Hold hands everyone!"

They quickly did as Grandma said and all held hands. Then they heard the 'pop' as they all disappeared from the room and found themselves hopping up and down on some very hot, nearly black-coloured sand. It was really the colour of ash. They all ran to the water's edge and breathed a sigh of relief when they felt the cool water on their hot feet.

"Where are we, Grandma?" asked Elise.

"We are in Martinique again, my darlings, and this is my favourite place in the whole world. It's called Saint-Pierre. See that mountain over there?" Grandma pointed to a tall mountain that didn't seem to be far away. They all nodded. Then she continued, "That mountain is a volcano and it's called Montagne Pelée."

It was all very strange for the children because one minute they were in Kent getting ready to go to sleep, and now here they were, on a sunny afternoon at the foot of an imposing volcano.

"But what's a volcano anyway?" they asked Grandma.

"Well," she started, "let's go and sit over here by this fishing boat."

The children had never seen a rowing boat before, except in pictures. Grandma looked around and spotted the fisherman dozing off in the shade of a hut covered with coconut branches. The hut was painted bright yellow with blue round the doorway and the window frames; only there was no door and no windows either! She went up to him, but the children remained where she had told them to wait. They couldn't make out what she was saying.

"I think that's French," said Elise to Coco. "I heard her say *bonjour*!"

"I think so too, Elise," said Coco. "I can speak French, you know."

"*Bonjour* Coco," said Elise with a giggle.

"*Bonjour* Elise," said Coco, "*comment ça va?*"

"Ça *va très bien*," replied Elise in a funny voice, and then they fell about laughing. The little ones were looking a bit confused.

Soon Grandma came back and said to them with a smile, "The fisherman said he would let us sit in his boat. Later he might take us for a little ride in it."

They squealed in delight and followed Grandma over to the boat. It looked very large and high. How would they get in? Grandma put her hand into her pocket and said, "Hold hands and close your eyes," which they did. The next thing they knew, they opened their eyes and found themselves in the boat. It was very strange.

As they sat down on the benches, Grandma started to tell them the story of the volcano and what happened on an awful day when the whole town was drowned in the really hot mud and lava that came out of the volcano mountain.

They were shocked and sad when they heard about

all the little children who had been gathered in the Cathedral for their First Holy Communion on the day the volcano erupted. "They are all little angels in Heaven," said Grandma, "and they went to heaven with their whole families, because they had all come to celebrate that day with them."

The children nodded their heads and thought about it.

"Shall we see if the fisherman can take us for that ride now?" asked Grandma

That cheered them up quite a bit and a little while later they were on the boat, in the middle of the bay, looking down at the shipwrecks that could be seen below.

When they got back to the shore, Grandma looked at her grandchildren.

"Shall we go back and see our family now?" asked Grandma gently. They all held hands and closed their eyes. Back at Grandma's house, they were very happy to see their mummies and gave them an extra special hug when they came into the room to kiss the children goodnight.

BLUE WATERS AND GOAT ISLAND

Several weeks had passed since the children had all been together at Grandma's house. This time they were celebrating the birthday of Didi, the cousin they saw the least often because she had been living in Africa.

Her mummy was a favourite of theirs because she was very good at making things and came up with great ideas for games to play.

So this was a very special weekend and Grandma's house was full of people – seven adults and six children. Everybody was excited, especially Coco and Louis, because although Didi had been in London for a whole week, this was their first chance to see her.

Luckily it was a beautiful day in June and it was practically warm! Summer seemed to be settling in for a little visit, with hours of sunshine, not much wind and lovely blue skies, with just one or two little cotton wool clouds floating around. That meant they could be out in the garden all day, playing on the swings, having a picnic on the grass and maybe even splashing in the little pool.

Grandpa put the deck chairs out on the grass and pulled out his barbecue to make yummy food later. He was just wiping the dew off the glass-topped table and chairs, the wooden picnic table and benches, as they all trooped downstairs for breakfast. They had arrived asleep last night so they had just found each other when they woke up that morning.

Grandma was in the kitchen making pancakes. She nearly always did when Coco and Louis came. Sometimes she made bakes, and they liked those too. But they loved the pancakes with syrup and were very happy. Coco called it 'makel' syrup.

They all climbed into chairs – everyone wanted to sit on a 'big chair' but Didi and Joe had to sit in the booster chairs so they could reach the table.

"There are six children sitting at the table," said Elise to no one in particular. She loved to say what was going on, so she continued, "One, two, three, four of us are sitting in big chairs and two are sitting in baby seats." Louis was proud to be sitting in a big chair.

"Who wants pancakes?" asked Grandma.

"Me! Me! Me!" they all shouted quite loudly.

"Not so loud, children – your mummies are sleeping."

"My mummy's awake," said Elise. "I went into her bed for a cuddle."

"My mummy's awake too," said Coco.

"Well, maybe they are trying to go back to sleep, so no more shouting. OK?"

"Yes Grandma," they chorused in their not-so-shouty voices.

"Who knows? If they are asleep when you finish breakfast, perhaps we can go on a little 'venture. Hmmm?" asked Grandma with a little wink.

"Yes! Yes!" Out came the shouty voices again. "Where are we going today, Grandma?"

"You'll see," Grandma said with a smile, "but first we have to tidy up."

When they had finished eating and helping Grandma tidy away the plates and cups, she gave each of them a little square of sponge so they could wipe off their place mats before putting them away. Soon the table was clear and clean and they all looked at Grandma.

"OK," said Grandma. "Come over here. Hold hands and close your eyes." She was waiting for them next to the beach with the glass dome top.

Didi and Joe didn't know what was going on, but they were very happy to hold hands with their cousins. Elise had to announce, "We're all in our pyjamas... we're not even dressed!"

"That's OK," said Grandma with a smile.

A quick 'pop' later and they opened their eyes to warm sun on a large, sandy beach! There was no one else around and the water was lovely and blue, and as flat as the glass in a mirror.

"This is Tobago," said Grandma, "and this beach is called Speyside. Do you see that big rock over there?"

She was pointing to a really big rock sitting out in the sea. "That rock is called Goat Island."

"Goat Island?" They all laughed at the name.

"Are there lots of goats on Goat Island?" asked Elise.

"Not at all," said Grandma, "but there are a lot of beautiful fish in the coral reefs around it."

"Hello there!" Suddenly they heard a voice. It was a rather weak and wobbly voice, and for a minute they weren't sure from where it had come. But then they heard it again. "Hello there!" and this time it went on, "Help me please!"

Grandma started looking around and, sure enough, behind a bush, there was a frail old man lying on his side in a little tidal pool, shivering violently. The children were a little scared but curious. Who was that? Why was he lying down in the water behind the bush? There was a little stream next to the bush that was flowing into the sea. They were at the far end of the bay. There were no houses nearby; at least they couldn't see any from the beach.

Grandma turned to the children and then said to Elise and Coco, "Girls, I want you to take care of Didi and Joe while I have a look at this old man and try to help him. OK?"

"Of course, Grandma," they both said together, and then they took Didi and Joe's hands in theirs and said, "Let's go play in the sand over here."

Grandma smiled at them as the two older girls shepherded the smaller ones over to the side and sat down in a circle to play in the sand.

Grandma then turned to the old man and said gently, "Why don't I help you to sit up?"

"I slipped and fell," the old man said. "I couldn't get up again."

"Well I am going to get help for you."

"If you help me stand, I will walk," he said.

So Grandma helped him to stand up. He did not look very steady. "Children!" called Grandma. "Please come and help me."

Nia came running up with Louis, and then Coco and Elise came, walking slowly with the two little ones who were all covered in sand. The children all gathered around Grandma and the old man, standing shakily with her help.

Coco took Didi's hand and Elise said, "I'm strong, Grandma. I will help him."

Elise held his other arm and looked up at the old man with a serious expression on her face. "We can help you, Mister," she said.

The old man took a deep breath and seemed to get stronger. "Thank you, young lady, he said in a quiet, gentle voice.

Together they all walked slowly along the beach for a few minutes. They saw a fishing boat coming in with two fishermen on board. Grandma said to the old man, "We will leave you now. These fishermen will help you."

She led him over to a coconut tree and he leaned against it gratefully. When he turned his head to thank them, they had disappeared.

Later that day, when he had dry clothes on and had eaten a bowl of good cowheel soup, he told his friends and his daughter about the lady and the six children who had rescued him, but nobody believed him. They thought he had dreamed it all. He thought then it may have been angels, because they had saved his life.

Just across the bay, on Goat Island, there were sounds of children giggling as they sat on an outcropping of rock and watched the brightly coloured fish cavorting around the beautiful coral in the clear water below…

MEETING ANNIE AND MAKING SAND CASTLES

Little Nia was crying because she had jumped/bounced off the bed at a bad angle and gone headfirst into the wall. She hit the wall so hard that there was a dent in the plaster the size of the lump on her head.

Her mummy was very scared and upset. She dashed down the stairs to get ice for a cold compress, leaving Elise to watch baby Joe and calling for Grandma to come. Nia was not enjoying the icy coldness on her forehead, no matter how many times her mummy said it would help with the lump!

She looked up and there was Grandma holding little Joe. Nia put on her saddest face. Grandma's face looked very worried as she asked gently, "How's my little head?"

Nia sniffed twice and then once more for effect and

said nothing. "Are you having Gregory compresses on your head?" asked Grandma, with a little twinkle in her eye.

Nia tried, but she could not stop her face from smiling a little as she remembered the little polar bear they had rescued from the iceberg on their last adventure. It had been very cold there and they had played with the snow and made snowballs. Now she could imagine that it was a snowball that Mummy was putting on her forehead. It didn't feel quite as cold as when it was just ice cubes in a wet towel.

Nia sat up a little and smiled a proper smile. "It's like a snowball, Grandma," she said and Grandma smiled too.

"Isn't it lucky that the rest of you is all nice and warm?"

"Yes, it is," agreed Nia.

"Are you OK now, darling?" asked Nia's mummy. Nia snuggled close to her mummy. She was OK, really, but she loved having cuddles with Mummy.

"I'm OK," she said after a minute.

"I have to take Joe upstairs to change his nappy," said Mummy. "You can have a cuddle with Grandma."

Nia glanced up sideways at Grandma who was smiling her little smile. "OK," said Nia, and she allowed her mummy to put her down. As soon as Mummy had taken Joe from Grandma, Nia took her grandma's hand and asked, "Grandma, do you want to watch me wave my flag? I made it at nursery today. The handle is a straw and it's a little bendy. We put sticky tape on it, but it's still bending a little."

Nia went over to the table and picked up her flag. It was very colourful. "I'm going to give it to Joe," she said.

"Oh, I'm sure he would like that," said Grandma.

"Do you want to have a go?" Nia asked Grandma in her very best sharing voice.

"Please, may I?" asked Grandma very politely.

"Here you go." Nia gave the flag to Grandma. "You have to hold it like this and wave it... let me show you." She took the flag back again and showed Grandma how to wave it.

"Where's Elise?" asked Grandma after a few waves of the flag.

"She's on the swings."

"Why don't we go and join her?" suggested Grandma.

"I don't want to swing, Grandma," said Nia in a voice that was a bit whiny.

"OK then. Shall we call Elise in and we can do something else all together?" asked Grandma.

"I'll get her Grandma," Nia said and she went out the patio door, which her sister had left ajar.

Grandma stopped by her Hawaiian beach for a moment and then went outside too.

At the bottom of the garden Elise was swinging higher and higher and having fun kicking at the apples on the apple tree opposite the swings. She was very good at swinging.

"Look at me, Grandma!" she squealed.

"You are almost reaching the sky," said Grandma.

"Look at me, Nia!" Elise squealed again.

"Come down, Elise," said Nia, "come off. I think Grandma has the magic shell in her pocket."

Elise didn't want to miss an adventure so she asked Grandma to help her stop the swing.

But Grandma laughed and a quick 'pop' later, Elise found herself swinging on a different swing next to a lovely beach on a bright, sunny day. She was wearing a swimming costume and so were Nia and Grandma.

Grandma's costume was a bit old-fashioned, thought Elise, but when she looked around, there was another group of people further along the beach and the adults were wearing the same kind of costume as Grandma.

A little girl came running down the beach to where they were. Elise jumped off the swing.

"Where did you come from?" the little girl asked.

"Well, good afternoon to you too!" said Grandma.

"What's your name?" the little girl asked Elise. Nia was being shy behind Grandma's legs.

"Elise," answered Elise. "What's yours? What happened to your hair?"

"My name is Annie. My hair fell out because of my med-i-cay-shun," the little girl said. "I have cancer."

Grandma looked on and smiled. *Children do not beat around the bush*, she thought, as a woman came up.

"That's my mummy," said Annie to the girls. "I have to go back to the hospital tomorrow."

"What's cancer?" asked Elise.

"It's when something goes wrong with your cells… Your mummy will explain it to you darling," said Grandma to Elise.

"It's nice to meet you, Annie," said Grandma to the little girl.

Then she said "Hello" to the little girl's mother, who looked very tired and sad. "Annie can play with us for a while, if you don't mind," Grandma went on in her gentle voice to the lady. "Don't worry, I will look after her."

The lady looked at Grandma for a moment and then sighed and smiled. "Oh thank you," she said. She looked like she was going to cry. "I'll just be over here, Annie," she said to the little girl.

"OK Mummy," Annie said.

"Do you like playing in the sand?" asked Elise.

"I like making castles," said the girl. "My mummy says soon I shall have my very own castle and I will be a princess."

So they sat down and made several castles using a castle-shaped bucket that had magically appeared next to them. After a long while Grandma said, "I think Annie is getting a bit tired, aren't you, Annie?"

Annie nodded her head. She didn't really want to stop playing with her new friends, but she was feeling rather tired and her head was starting to hurt.

Grandma took Annie's hand and Elise took her other hand. Nia held Grandma's other hand and they all walked slowly down the beach to where Annie's mummy and daddy were. They said goodbye and, after a while when Annie looked down the beach, she thought she saw them disappear.

But she didn't tell her mummy. She just smiled and thought, *They must have been those angels that Mummy said would come to help me not be afraid.* She sighed a big sigh and fell asleep on her mummy's shoulder.

Elise was back on her own swings. "Grandma," she said, "I liked Annie."

"I know darling," said Grandma. "I think she liked you too."

"What was the name of that beach, Grandma?" asked Elise.

"That beach was called Sans Souci and it is on the north coast of the island of Trinidad. Sans Souci means 'No worries.'"

"Is that the real name?" asked Elise.

"Oh yes, it is," answered Grandma.

"That little girl was really very sick, wasn't she?" Elise was very thoughtful.

"Yes, darling, but you know, girls, you cheered her up and it's always nice to cheer up people who are feeling poorly."

Elise and Nia nodded.

"… And you must remember her always," said Grandma. "Look, there is your mummy calling you in for dinner."

Elise and Nia came off the swings and holding hands, they slowly walked back up the garden together. They were all thinking of Annie…

THE OCTOBER BIRTHDAYS
AND THE JELLYFISH BEACH

Once again, all of the cousins were together at Grandma's house for a birthday. This time it was Nia's birthday. The family called this celebration 'The October birthdays' because it was a party shared by Grandma, Taty Zou and Nia, who all had their birthdays in October, only days apart. Nia loved her birthday celebration because there were always three cakes and lots of lovely food and spoily presents.

This one was lovely. Even though it had been rainy and windy and generally autumn-type weather, the day of the party was dry and sunny, and all the trees were beautiful and dressed in gold and orange and red. It was Saturday and the children had all slept together on Friday night without knowing it. Taty Zou lived the farthest and liked to make her long drive with sleeping, quiet children. They were then popped into bed at Grandma's house and almost like magic, woke up with all their cousins!

They were all excited and happy to be together and there was a lot of fun sharing going on. Nobody was being selfish and they were having a lovely time.

Downstairs their mummies, daddies, Grandma and Grandpa were enjoying the moment too. The babies had gone back to sleep, so it was really quiet and relaxing… but not for long. There was a noise like a herd of elephants approaching. Was it elephants? No! It was the four older cousins coming downstairs for breakfast.

Grandma was all ready for them with the pancake batter on the side and the pans on the stove. She flicked on the burners under the pans and stood there, spatula in hand, ready to make delicious pancakes for breakfast. The children trooped in and soon were seated around the table. They could smell pancakes.

"Grandma's pancakes! Yay!" Elise clapped her hands and all the children chorused, "Grandma's pancakes! Yay!"

Of course all this noise woke the babies, but they were soon smiling and giggling because they loved being with the older children and they quite liked a bit of pancake too!

"I am going to stuff myself with pancakes," announced Elise.

"Me too! Me too!" chorused the other children and the babies waved their arms around and giggled to show they agreed.

Grandma had three frying pans on the stove and was

making pancakes as fast as she could to feed these hungry little people. Very often Grandpa made pancakes too, but his were always a lavish affair, with bacon and eggs as well.

Grandma had crushed a couple of very ripe bananas into the pancake batter and the lovely odour of caramelised banana was making everyone's mouth water. She was also making blueberry pancakes!

The children kept asking for more and more and more, until their mummies thought they would burst.

Grandpa came in and did one of his growly bear noises and all the children squealed. They loved their grandpa – he always growled and tried to catch and tickle them. He also provided paper for drawing and making aeroplanes and, at the old house, he had bought them a huge tub of crayons.

Elise particularly liked sneaking into his office, because he often had his telly on in there. He loved to cook and he did the best barbecues and hot dogs. He made them laugh when he chased away a squirrel or a magpie trying to get at the seeds he put out for the birds. He loved the tiny little birds, and there was one robin that knew him. It would hop over and cock its head at him as if to say, "Go on, let's have some yummy seeds then!"

Grandma and the mummies were going to be busy today making food and cakes. Coco and Louis' mummy had already made lots of yummy fairy cakes and Nia's mummy was probably going to make her lovely muffins. Didi's mummy, Taty Lidi, often made and always decorated the birthday cakes.

Grandpa was going to barbecue because the weather

looked pretty good and Grandma would probably make macaroni pie and her colourful Spanish rice (and probably her callaloo, which the children were not sure they liked before they tasted the yummy spinach dish; they always needed coaxing from their mummies!). Maybe there would be some ice cream too.

Elise was very excited. She quite liked sweet things, but her mummy only let her have a little bit on special days like birthdays because they made her go a little crazy. She felt like a bouncy ball whenever she had sweet things; she couldn't stop bouncing up and down.

Nia was looking forward to the cakes. There were always lots of candles to blow out and she loved being in between Grandma and Taty Zou while everybody sang 'Happy Birthday' to them all.

When the mummies went upstairs to have a shower and change, Grandma looked at her six grandchildren and smiled a happy smile. She loved having them all around together.

"Shall we nip off for a quick adventure, children?"

Grandpa was out in the garden getting his barbecue going and all the food was ready. Nia's godmother, Aunty Janet, hadn't yet arrived.

"Yes! Yes! Please Grandma," squealed the children all together. Little Didi and Joe clapped hands.

"OK then," said Grandma.

"We know, Grandma," said Coco, "we hold hands and close our eyes!" which they all did and 'pop', they heard the magic sound.

When they opened their eyes, they were on a strange

beach that seemed to stretch on for miles in both directions. On the horizon where the sea met the sky, they could see lots of large ships.

"Where are we, Grandma?" asked Nia. Every single one of the children had been wondering the same thing.

"Well, do you remember your Bible stories – the one where Moses parted the Red Sea to help the people escape from the Egyptian soldiers?"

"Yes, I remember, I remember!" shouted Elise and Coco and Nia all together.

"I 'member too!" said Louis, but he probably didn't.

Grandma smiled and, looking out to sea said, "Well, this is the Red Sea!"

The children were amazed. Sometimes they thought that the Bible stories were pretend, so they were amazed to know that the Red Sea actually existed.

"Why are there so many boats on the Red Sea, Grandma?" asked Coco, with a frown.

"They are all waiting to go through the Suez Canal," said Grandma.

"What's the Suez Canal?" asked Elise.

"Well, many, many years ago, some people wanted to find a quick way to get to the Mediterranean Sea, so they cut a passage between the Red Sea and the Mediterranean Sea. That way they wouldn't have to go all the way around Africa any more. Instead of spending weeks at sea, they can get through in a few days."

"Grandma, Grandma! Look!" squealed Louis and Nia. They were pointing to the wet sand where the gentle waves had washed up some strange-looking things on the beach.

"What is that, Grandma?" asked Nia, screwing up her face. "It looks yucky."

"Those are jellyfish," said Grandma. "We won't be going into the sea with those around."

"Why not, Grandma? Why can't we go in the water?" asked Coco and Elise, disappointed.

"Jellyfish can sting you if you touch them," explained Grandma, "it feels like fire. The problem is you can't see them very well when they are in the water. Look at how you can see right through them. They're made of jelly."

"Like the kind you eat?" asked Louis. He was not at all sure they were made of yummy jelly.

Grandma laughed. "No, darling, not like the kind you eat. But they do look like gelatine, which is what jelly is made of."

"Yucch! Yucky!" squealed the kids. Then they started running up to the beached jellyfish and running away again, squealing "Yucch! Yucky!" They forgot about their disappointment at not being able to swim in the sea and had a great time scaring themselves with the big, floppy white blobs of 'jelly' that littered the beach.

Didi and Joe dug in the sand and found some shells.

They were all happy to find themselves back at Grandma's house later. They were hungry and there was a birthday cake, birthday muffins *and* birthday cupcakes to eat!

Nia enjoyed her birthday a lot, and they all played jellyfish in the bath that evening before climbing into bed to talk about the 'venture they had had that day...

THE BEACH IN THE WOOD

One day all the cousins were having fun and playing together at Grandma's house. It was a special day – Grandpa's birthday. All their mummies were there to wish their own daddy a happy birthday, and Grandma had made all the special foods Grandpa loved to eat.

There was curried chicken and goat and shrimps. There was roti (dahlpuri) and buss-up-shut (paratha). These were two different kinds of indian bread. There was curried channa (chick peas) and spicy okras, aubergine and large bodi (runner beans). There was curried potato (the indian name for that was 'aloo') and fluffy white rice. There would be coconut ice cream for dessert and lovely mango too. And a birthday cake for later. Everyone would be stuffed.

The cousins were really happy because their friends Nathan and his twin brothers Zachary and Josh were there with their parents too. They were considered to be part of the family. Of course they had never all been on a 'special beach adventure' together, because it would have been very hard not to notice if *nine* children suddenly disappeared... especially if this were to happen on Grandpa's birthday!

So the children were very surprised when Grandma said, "Let's all get our coats and wellies on and go looking for a beach!"

The children laughed and Elise said, "Grandma, you know there aren't any beaches near here! The sea is very far away from here!"

"Just get dressed and come with me," said her Grandma. "You'll see."

All the children scuttled around, laughing at their funny grandma, who was going to go looking for a beach, when they knew that the only places to go near her house were the woods and the playground. Still, they always had fun with their grandma, so they got their wellies on, put on their coats and buttoned them up too, because it was November and very cold and damp.

Grandma shushed everyone and opened the door. The children could hear their mummies and daddies chatting in the living room. Grandpa had put some music on. She called to them, "The children are just going out for some fresh air with me!"

Various "OK"s came back from the living room where they seemed to be having a lively discussion.

Once they closed the front door behind them, they knew what to do. Older children held hands with the younger ones and they moved off like a little army, chattering happily.

Elise and Coco were at the front, each holding hands with the youngest cousins, Didi and Joe. Nia and Louis followed, holding hands. Then came Grandma with the twins and Nathan.

Elise was now nine and Coco was eight. Nia was seven and Louis was nearly six. Didi and Joseph were four. Nathan was seven, while the twins were five. They were all used to going for walks with Grandma and always behaved like little angels. That made their parents very proud and happy when Grandma told them how good their children had been.

They stopped for a few minutes to watch the stream come out from under the bridge and Grandma exclaimed at how much water there was. "We'll have a twig race on the way back," she said. "Let's keep going. We mustn't stay out too late."

The children obediently started walking again and soon came to the entrance to the woods.

"Can we do echoes, please Grandma?" Coco and Elise asked.

"Yes of course you can, but be careful where you walk because it might be slippery."

"Yay!" they shouted and headed off into the little tunnel under the train line, shouting "Woo-woo" and laughing at the echoes that came back.

Nathan looked at Grandma and she smiled, "Of course you can go too, Nathan. You too, boys," she told the twins, who were still holding hands. Off they shot.

She stood back for a while, because they were making lots of noise. Then she strode in and held out her hands. They all knew this was the signal to go, and they formed up again to continue tramping into the wood.

"Girls," called Grandma, "do you see that path over to the right? Let's go there."

The girls obediently turned off onto that path and everybody followed, until they came to a clearing. It was very pebbly underfoot and there was very little grass or anything growing on the ground. It was a strange space in the middle of the woods. There was usually grass and little wild flowers and weeds growing everywhere. They could hear the little stream on the other side of the clearing and see the trees and plants on the banks of the stream.

"Hold hands everyone and close your eyes!" said Grandma suddenly and the bigger children did as they were told. The twins had to be persuaded to close their eyes, but as soon as they did, there was a little 'pop'. When the children opened their eyes, their mouths opened too – the stream had turned into a river and they were standing on the seashore, watching the river empty itself into a flat, flat sea.

"Where did the trees go?" asked Nathan.

"We are in another place," explained Coco.

Elise added, "A special secret place that only Grandma knows."

"Look at all the pebbles and shells," exclaimed Nia. "Let's collect some."

"I want to splash in the water!" said Louis.

"Go on then," said Grandma with a gentle smile, "but don't go too far from Grandma. Promise?"

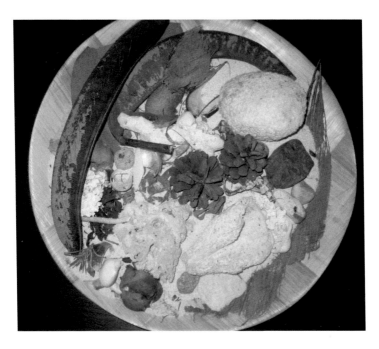

Barbados

Black sand beach, Martinique

Chatelaillon, France

Grandma at Les Salines

Grandma's first beach

Green waters, Maqueripe Trinidad

Gulf of Paria, Trinidad

La Romaine

La Romaine

Magical beach, Hawaii

Petrified Savannah, St Anne,
Martinique

Pink sand beach, Barbados

Red Sea, Egypt

Salines, Martinique

Tobago

The Beach Collection

"Yes, Grandma!" said Louis and he started splashing in the water. As he was still holding Nathan and Josh's hands, they went off together. Zach collected shells with Nia.

Elise and Coco, who were always together, decided to take a closer look at the river. Grandma stayed close and kept her eye on all the children.

It was cold, but there was a watery sun beginning to go down, and strange birds flew around in circles, looking for fish in the shallow water.

"Be careful children," called Grandma, "those birds are hungry and they won't appreciate it if you scare away all the fishes!"

After a little while, the children all gathered around Grandma.

"This place, children, was here before the woods. The river kept washing the earth from its banks and depositing it here where it meets the sea. For hundreds of years this place filled with earth and pushed back the sea, until one day, the birds ate fruits and dropped the seeds here. The seeds grew into plants and trees and the woods were formed. The great river became that tiny little stream."

"Is that how all woods are made? Was the sea everywhere before?"

"No, my darlings, not all woods, but this one. The land is shaped in lots of different ways. Sometimes water shapes the land by wearing it away. Sometimes water shapes the land by moving dirt and sand from one place to another. Sometimes it breaks rocks into sand, and sometimes it drains away and leaves sand and mud to turn hard and become rock!"

"Water can break rocks?" Louis wasn't sure about that.

"Yes, it can, by seeping into cracks and wearing down the rock until the rock cracks open. But it takes a very long time, rolling rocks around until they get smaller and smaller or knock against each other so often that they crack and break up. Water can move away small stones and earth that hold a rock in place until that rock rolls away one day and crushes others on its way. All these changes can take years and years and years, more than a hundred years, sometimes."

Louis thought about that for a long time as he kicked a pebble around.

"But you know," Grandma added gently, "water does not work alone. Every element of nature works in harmony with the others and in different forms. Who can tell me the different forms water can take?"

"I know," squealed Elise. "Rain!"

"And ice," said Coco.

And it can be a river or a waterfall or a stream," added Grandma.

"Or the sea!" said Nia.

"That's right," said Grandma. "And who knows the name of the other elements?"

"Elements? What are elements?" asked Nia.

"Well, there are four main elements and they are fire, water, earth and wind," said Grandma. They all nodded and tried to remember. "Time to go home, children; don't forget your pebbles and shells. Hold hands and close your eyes. We still have to walk home when we get back to our wood. Then we'll have hot choc."

They all held hands and were glad to be going back home for hot chocolate. They took one last look at the setting sun and they closed their eyes and heard the 'pop'. When they opened their eyes, they were standing in the clearing in the wood, not far from the little gurgling stream. They had had an interesting adventure and the stream looked different to them now. The pebbles too, on which they stood. They headed back to Grandma's house and on the way they talked about what fire and wind and water and earth could do.

The little ones were tired and wanted their mummies. Grandma could only carry two of them but luckily, her house was very close by and soon enough they were curled up on the floor, eating bread and butter and drinking hot chocolate.

"Had a nice tramp in the woods with Grandma?" Coco's mummy asked.

"Yes," answered Coco, showing her the pebbles and shells she had collected. "Look at what I found."

"You found shells in the woods?" her mummy asked, surprised.

"Well, it used to be by the sea once long ago," replied Coco. "Didn't you know?"

LITTLE BACOLET BEACH

This time Grandma, Elise, Nia, Coco and Louis were on a small, curved beach, bordered with tall coconut trees. The sand was warm and sandy coloured, but there weren't many shells. What caught their attention was the way in which the big waves crashed on the shore over and over again.

"Look up there," said Grandma to the children, "that's the Bluehaven Hotel. We used to live there when your mummies were little girls. As a matter of fact, that was your Taty Lidi's first home. She came here when she was only three days old."

The children looked up at the long, two-storied building that curved along the top of the hill overlooking the bay.

"What's this place called, Grandma?" asked Elise.

"It's called Little Bacolet Bay," Grandma answered.

"Is there a Big Bacolet Bay, Grandma?" asked Coco.

"As a matter of fact, there is, darling. When Grandma was a little girl, her very best friend, Kamy, lived on Big Bacolet Bay with her family. Grandma used to come and spend some of her holidays there. Kamy and I used to clamber all over the rocks and look at the little crabs. Do you know, those crabs could hold onto the rock so hard that even one of those big waves couldn't wash them away!"

The children looked at the rocks on either side of the little bay and thought their grandma must have been a very brave little girl indeed.

"Could we go on the rocks, Grandma?" asked Nia. "I know I could climb on them and hold on really tight so the waves couldn't wash me away!"

"Not today, Nia. I thought we could just sit and watch the big waves for a while and then maybe we could even go in and have a play with the smaller ones."

The children looked at the big waves with their eyes as large as saucers. "Go in there??" asked Coco in an incredulous voice (she couldn't believe what Grandma was saying could be true).

"Yes, my dear; but first we must look at the waves."

"They look angry," said Elise to no one in particular. She did that a lot, just saying her thoughts out loud. Sometimes it got her into trouble, but not today.

"I suppose they do look a bit angry. Is that how you feel sometimes, Elise, when you get angry?"

"Yes," said Elise. "I want to crash down like that big wave!"

"But look closely, darling," said Grandma in her

gentlest voice. "Look at what happens after the wave crashes down."

"It's not angry anymore," said Elise with a little smile.

"And it's really gentle, rolling up the shore," continued Grandma, "until it's a playful little ripple, tickling your toes and then running away back into the sea. Maybe you could try to think of a wave when you get angry, and you could try being a gentle ripple. As you see, the wave doesn't stay angry for long."

"I'll try that, Grandma," said Elise, looking at the waves rising, crashing, then rolling gently up the sand to where they were sitting.

"Can we go and play in the ripples?" asked Coco.

"Yes, please can we go, Grandma?" everyone was saying all together.

Grandma laughed, "Yes, why don't we go and play tag with the ripples. But careful, don't go out to where the big waves are crashing."

"We'll be careful, Grandma," said the children together.

Then they all went and started playing in the shallows, where the waves that were once big and angry were rushing gently up the beach, trying to tickle their toes…

That night, the children were all tucked up in bed and falling asleep, after a very rowdy bathtime, where they pretended to be big waves crashing and then gentle ripples tickling.

Little Didi and Joe giggled madly when their toes were tickled and they all laughed a lot.

As for Grandma, she went off to her favourite chair in the living room to have a snooze.

GREGORY

Elise and Nia were giggling in the back seat of Grandma and Grandpa's car. They were going somewhere without their mummy and they did not know where. It was very exciting. Grandma said it would be a nice surprise.

"Are we going to see Gregory?" asked Elise suddenly after they had been driving for a while.

"I suppose we could have done that," said Grandma, "but I don't have my magic with me."

"Oh," said Elise, disappointed. "Can we go back home and get it?"

"No, darling, we cannot. We have been in the car for half an hour already, so we are too far away to go back now," said Grandma in her gentle voice.

Nia had fallen asleep and just then gave a little snore.

"Shhhh!" whispered Grandma to Elise, "why don't you have a little sleep and when we get there I will wake you up. You'll see, you will be very happy when we get there."

Elise started to say, "But Grandma…" in a grumpy voice, but Grandma shushed her again and she stopped. She sat for a minute and realised that she was quite sleepy after all. In one minute her eyes had closed and she was fast asleep.

Then suddenly she was not asleep anymore, because Grandma's voice was waking her up and she could hear another voice saying, "Elise! Elise! Hello Elise! Hello Nia!" It was Coco.

That was the surprise. They had come to Rat's Castle to see their cousins, Coco and Louis, their Uncle Hugo and Taty Zou.

Just for a moment, Elise wondered if there were once lots of rats at Rat's Castle. Had there been a King and Queen Rat and maybe Prince and Princess Rats? She thought she would ask Coco one day, but not right now. They were getting out of the car and Coco was already wanting Elise to come and play in the garden.

It was a lovely sunny day and the children all ran off together, laughing, as soon as Elise and Nia had got down from the car. They were wide awake now!

They played on the swings and the slide. They climbed up and down the climbing frame. Then Coco's mummy suggested they go cherry picking and they all trooped off with baskets to the cherry orchard, to pick lots of lovely cherries. Grandma loved cherries and she was just as excited as the children.

They had a good time picking cherries, but the baskets

did not get very full. Too much cherry munching had been going on. They were all stuffed with lovely sweet cherries, and a couple of T-shirts did get more than a little stained. Oh well! That's cherry picking for you.

They trudged back up the lane, keeping safely to the side in case a car should come along.

When they got back to the house they laid out on a blanket on the grass for a little rest. Taty Zou, Grandpa and Uncle Hugo all went off to make lunch, and Grandma stayed with the children out on the grass. After a little rest, the children got up and came over to where Grandma was sitting.

"Grandma," they said, "what shall we do now?"

"Well, we shall be having lunch very soon. Shall we have a story?"

"Oh yes, please," they all said together.

"Let's see! What shall it be? Hmmm!" Grandma frowned and thought very hard. "I know," she said. "Let's go and sit over there in the shade."

They all went off to the side of the house with Grandma and then sat down again in the shade.

"Do you remember when I told you about Gregory?" asked Grandma.

"Yes, I do!" cried Elise. "I do! He's a polar bear and he was lost on an iceberg and all alone."

"I wish we could see him," said Nia.

"Well, guess what I've just found in my pocket," said Grandma with a cheeky smile.

"Your magic shell!" cried Coco. "It's your magic shell, isn't it Grandma?" She jumped up and down and all the other children jumped up and down too. There were only four of them, because Didi and Joe had not come. They were with their mummies doing something else.

"Hold hands and close your eyes then," said Grandma, "we can't be gone long because it's nearly time for lunch."

The children did as they were told and heard the little 'pop'. They were amazed when they opened their eyes again. This was a strange beach indeed. It was really cold and they were glad to be wearing furry hoods and thick coats.

Everywhere they looked there was ice and water… except for a medium-sized polar bear with tears in his eyes. It was Gregory, and he was looking very forlorn indeed.

"Where's your mummy?" exclaimed Coco.

Gregory wasn't quite sure what to make of these small, strange-looking creatures who were making peculiar noises at him. But it was also very nice not to be all alone. He wondered if they had any food… he was very hungry. Most of all, he missed his mummy.

Polar bears eat just about everything – berries, fish, even penguins, but there weren't any of those around. Gregory was only little, so he couldn't take care of himself. Besides, he was stuck on a little iceberg, with nothing and no one else on it. He was feeling a little weak and very sad.

Grandma put one of her hands into the pocket of her coat and brought out some berries. Gregory caught sight of them and made a little grunty noise. Grandma walked over to him slowly, with her hand outstretched. When she got close, he nuzzled her hand and ate the berries.

"Can I feed him? Can I feed him?" squealed Elise. She stopped when Gregory looked scared at the noise. "Can I feed him Grandma?" she asked again in a quieter voice.

"I want to feed him," said Louis, peeking round from where he was hiding behind Grandma.

Soon all the children were feeding Gregory berries and biscuits and bits of bread that they found in their coat pockets.

After a while Coco said, "We can't leave him here all alone, Grandma. He looks so sad."

"He needs his mummy," said Nia in a voice full of concern.

"He wants his mamma," said Louis.

"That's true," said Grandma. "Shall we try and find his mummy then?"

"Yes! Yes!" chorused the children, but then they looked around and Elise said, "How will we find her, Grandma?"

"Grandma can use her magic, Elise," said Coco knowingly.

"Well, I've never done this before," said Grandma, thinking hard. "Hush now, let me think."

They all shushed one another and looked at Grandma expectantly.

"OK," said Grandma, "everyone hold hands and include Gregory in our circle."

They did as they were told and 'pop', they opened their eyes to see a hill covered in snow, with a very large polar bear at the top of it. She was shaking her head and looked at the little group in surprise. Then she started lumbering down the side of the hill because she could see Gregory, her baby who had been lost when the iceberg broke off and drifted away.

"Quick, children," said Grandma, "we have to go now. Gregory will be fine with his mummy."

"Can we say goodbye to Gregory?" asked Elise.

"Go on then, but be quick. His mummy is rather large and she might not understand what you are doing with her baby."

They all gave Gregory a quick hug and a pat and he made one of his little grunty noises. They held hands, closed their eyes and heard the 'pop' just as a rather large polar bear came crashing down to where Gregory was.

"Whew, that was close!" exclaimed Coco, when they found themselves sitting on the grass again. "Shall we tell my mummy about Gregory?"

"Go right ahead!" smiled Grandma, leaning back and closing her eyes. She knew what her daughter would think when she heard the story. Her secret magic was quite safe.

"That wasn't really a beach, Grandma," said Coco. "There weren't any shells or sand or pebbles."

"There are a million different kinds of beaches in the world, my Coco," said Grandma in her really quiet voice.

The children looked at Grandma and Coco put her fingers to her lips. "Shhh!" she said.

"Grandma's having a little nap," said Nia.

"Let's go and play," said Elise.

"I want to see my mummy," said Louis.

"I'll take you to see her," said Nia, holding his hand, and off they went.

Grandma heard Elise squeal a moment later, "Mummy!"

She smiled. Her other daughter had arrived and they would all be together for a lovely afternoon in the sun.

12

BACK TO LA ROMAINE-ON-SEA

The children looked around and not all of them recognised the place where they were. They were halfway down a slope, where lots of tufts of reeds and grass clung to the dry earth. All of it looked like it was about to tumble into the sea, which lapped gently at the bottom. Looking up they could see a few tall trees, whose long, exposed roots hung temptingly down like ropes in a strange playground.

"I know this place! I know this place!" said Coco excitedly. "It's Grandma's beach when she was a little girl!"

"… When she was a little girl??!" echoed Elise and Nia together.

"Yes, and she was here. She showed it to me," cried Coco. "Grandma – well, little girl Grandma I mean – was here. We went for a walk on the muddy beach and found a little coconut tree."

"I wish I could see Grandma, I mean little girl

Grandma," said Nia and then they all suddenly looked around again as a thought dawned on them. Where *was* Grandma? Normally, when they popped into one of their 'ventures, on a beach somewhere in the world, Grandma was always with them. But they could not see her anywhere today; they were all alone.

"Where shall we go?" asked Elise.

"Why don't you come up here!" shouted a voice suddenly. They looked up, squinting their eyes against the glare.

"It's her! It's her!" cried Coco to Elise and Nia and Louis and Didi and Joe. "It's little girl Grandma!"

Elise and Nia felt a little shy all of a sudden, but really excited too. The little ones, Louis and Didi and Joe, did not understand and looked very confused. Everything was very, very strange.

"Come on!" said Coco, holding out her hand to her little brother. Elise held out her hand to her little brother Joe and Nia held out her hand to Didi. Then together, they all started up the slope. It was not very far to the top, but it looked quite steep.

"Don't look down," little girl Grandma called out. "Here, I'll help you." She held out her hands and they all felt like they were floating. In no time they were standing in a circle around the girl. One by one they looked curiously at her and, one by one, they recognised the twinkly eyes and gentle smile. It really *was* Grandma! Elise's eyes were as wide as saucers and Nia couldn't say a word.

"Hello again!" said the little girl to Coco. "Do you remember me? My name is Toni." Coco nodded.

Just then, a voice rang out. "Toni!"

"Yes, Mummy," answered Toni. "Coming Mummy."

"You can come with me," she told the children, "it's my mummy calling. She would love to meet you."

The children looked at one another and nodded. "OK," they all said.

"It's just over here," said Toni. "Mummy never likes to be where she cannot see the sea."

Soon they were standing with Toni in front of an older woman. She was smiling and they could not help smiling back. She was not very tall, with light brown skin, twinkly eyes and the kindest smile.

"I just made some guava cheese," she said. "Children, would you like to taste some?"

"Yes, please," the children answered politely.

They couldn't help staring at Grandma/Toni's mummy.

"What can we call her?" whispered Coco to Toni.

"Oh, Granny, I guess. That's what your mummy calls her."

"Does my mummy know her?" asked Elise, feeling a little bolder now.

"Of course she does," said Toni. "She's her grandmother too. Your mummies used to spend a lot of time here when they were little."

"Here?!" Coco and Elise exclaimed together, looking around curiously.

"Well, at the house over there, with my mummy and daddy, and outside in the garden too. They had a lot of fun here in La Romaine."

"Did they go down to the sea with, er, Granny?" asked

Coco and she was a little surprised when Grandma/Toni shook her head.

"I don't think so. My daddy used to drive all the way across the island to a beach called Benitier, in Mayaro. Do you remember? That's the first beach where you had an adventure."

"I remember," said Coco, "but Elise wasn't there that time. There was a monkey."

"That's true," said Grandma/Toni, smiling. "Maybe we will all go there again sometime, but my mummy and daddy can only be here, in La Romaine… and me too." She sounded a little wistful.

"Didn't you have any sisters and brothers?" asked Elise.

"No," answered Grandma/Toni. "I was on my own. But I had a lot of dogs."

"Yes, you said you used to take your dogs down to the beach to swim in the sea," said Coco. "Where are your dogs, Gra…, I mean Toni?"

"Would you like to meet them?" asked Toni.

"Oh yes, please," said the children all together.

Grandma/Toni whistled. Suddenly there were dogs everywhere. She introduced them one by one.

"This black and white spotted one is Bella, she's the oldest. These two, Debi and Fido are her pups." She was pointing to two brown and white dogs who looked very playful. "Then this black one here is Kippy," said Toni, pointing to a funny-looking dog with very short legs. "He's very fierce and doesn't like strangers… but don't worry. He won't bite you if he knows you are my friends. I have two other dogs, but they have to be kept tied up, because they are Alsatian guard dogs."

"What are their names?" asked Elise.

"Diane and Quicky," replied Toni.

"Is Quicky very quick?" asked Coco.

"Just at eating his food," laughed Toni. "He's still only a puppy really. Diane is his mummy. She's really the oldest because I got her when she was a little puppy. She was given to me as a birthday present when I was one!"

"Gosh! You sure have a lot of dogs!" said Nia in wonder.

"They are my friends. They go everywhere with me… except school of course, and church!"

"Here, children, come and taste my guava cheese," said Granny, "but be careful and don't let the dogs steal it from you." She handed around pieces of the dark fruit 'cheese', which had been rolled in sugar.

"It was nice to meet you, children," said Toni's mummy. "I have to go and make supper now. Do come again soon. Toni, don't be too long."

"Your mummy makes sweets! You are so lucky," Elise said to Toni. "I like that guava cheese."

"When you come again, you can try her breadfruit flower candy," smiled Toni. "That's very nice too. I have to go now. I hope you will come again. You should all hold hands now," Toni said and, for a moment, she sounded just like Grandma.

They held hands and 'pop', they were in the garden at Grandma's house, down by the swings. Grandma was walking back up to the house.

"Shall we play on the swings for a little while?" asked Coco.

Didi and Joe toddled off after their grandma, leaving

the older children to play on the swings and talk a bit about the 'venture they had just had with little girl Grandma. They couldn't tell anyone else about their secret adventures.

13

THE BEACH AT HALF MOON BAY

All the children were together again. They were at Rat's Castle with Coco's mummy and daddy. They had spent an hour in the pool and Coco was showing her cousins all her swimming skills. She really was a good swimmer and all those swimming lessons were showing. Louis and the girls were jumping into the pool and making big splashes. It was a lovely day.

Grandma and Grandpa were not with them, nor was Taty Lidi or Didi, who were far away in West Africa. However, it was June and Didi and her mummy would be coming very soon and then they would be getting together at Grandma and Grandpa's house to celebrate Didi's birthday again.

Elise and Nia loved coming to Rat's Castle for two reasons. First of all it was because Coco and Louis were there and they loved being with their cousins. Secondly,

Rat's Castle had great gardens – they could play on the swings and go up and down the ladder to the open platform at the top that doubled most days as the deck of a pirate ship. They could swim in the pool and play golf, and just generally run around like crazy.

When it was cherry season it was even nicer because they got to go cherry picking with Taty Zou and Uncle Hugo. It was truly great, especially if it was a sunny day. Their Uncle Hugo was loads of fun and Taty Zou too. They didn't miss their mummy one little bit.

At the end of the day they were tired after running around, and climbing, and playing pirates, and golf and splashing in the pool. They had left baby Joe with Mummy. Taty Zou called them in for dinner. She had made lovely butternut squash soup and all the children tucked in like starving people who had not eaten in days. They wolfed down the delicious soup with chunks of bread and butter. Then they had yogurt pots and a piece of fruit for dessert. Yumm!

Then... Mummy turned up to take Elise and Nia back home.

"Where's Grandma? Is she coming too?" asked Elise.

"No, darling," said Mummy, "but we'll be seeing her and Grandpa as soon as we get back home. Isn't it lucky that we all live together?"

"Yes, I like having Grandma and Grandpa with us. Grandpa loves to scare us. He's so much fun and Grandma gives really nice cuddles," said Elise.

"And she makes pancakes!" said Nia.

The cousins didn't want to part, but they had spent a

lovely day together and their mummies said they could come back to Rat's Castle another day. So they hugged and kissed each other goodbye. Coco kissed baby Joe, who had come with Taty Tsui, and hugged Nia. She kissed Taty Tsui and then hugged and kissed Elise. Louis was being a bit shy, but he kissed Taty Tsui and said a quiet "Bye" to Elise and Nia, and a special "Bye baby Joe" to his little cousin Joe. Then, their mummies hugged and kissed each other four times (two kisses on each cheek) before putting Elise, Nia and Joe into the car.

"So, did you have a nice day at Rat's Castle?" asked Mummy.

"Yes," said Elise and Nia together. Then they took it in turns to tell their mummy all they had done. Joe fell asleep.

When Elise and Nia got home they were almost asleep. In fact they had both dozed off in the car for a little while, but they woke up when the car stopped and Mummy opened the door. They climbed out of their seats and slowly made their way to the front door while Mummy got Joe out. They knocked on the door and Grandpa came to the door.

"Who's there?" he growled in his deep voice.

"Elise and Nia," said Elise and Nia together with a giggle.

"Should I let you in?" growled Grandpa.

"Yes," they both shouted, "let us in!"

Grandpa opened the door and welcomed them in with a big smile. They scuttled past him and ran into the living room, squealing in excitement, "Grandpa's coming! Grandpa's coming!"

Then they saw their Grandma sitting in her favourite chair. They ran to her and climbed into her lap. "Save us, Grandma!" they squealed.

Grandma sighed and gave Grandpa a stern look. "Now, now!" she said in her quiet voice. "Let's all calm down. It's nearly bedtime."

Grandpa went over to the fridge and opened it. The children calmed down a little.

Grandma asked them if they had enjoyed their visit to their cousins Coco and Louis. They nodded and then both started to tell Grandma what they had done.

"Well," said Grandma, "I suppose you've had enough excitement and adventures for one day."

The children looked at her and they knew what she meant. Whenever Grandma talked about adventures, it always meant that a beach adventure could be coming. The children loved their beach 'ventures with their grandma and her magic.

"Let's get you to bed," said Grandma, lifting the girls off her lap and setting them down on the floor. Then she stood up and looked around. They were all alone in the living room because their mummy had gone straight upstairs with baby Joe and Grandpa had gone back into his office and closed the door. She cocked her head to one side and looked at them.

"Shall we have a quick 'venture before bed?" she asked, knowing the answer already.

"Yes! Yes!" said Elise and Nia together.

Grandma wasted no time in getting her shell and 'pop', they found themselves on a beautiful beach that stretched around a bay, which curved in a perfect semi-circle.

"This is Half Moon Bay, girls," Grandma said. "The water is lovely and warm so you can have a little swim if you like."

"What country is this?" asked Elise.

"This is an island called Antigua," said Grandma. "After your swim we'll go and have a look around."

The girls ran into the water and it was lovely and warm. There were no people on the beach at all and what looked like a hotel on the shore was empty and deserted.

"Why are there no people here, Grandma?" asked Elise when they came out of the water.

"Well, they have gone away to another beach," said Grandma. "This place is another one of my favourite places in the world, but the people who used to be here ran out of money and ideas. They needed lots of people to come and stay at their hotel, and when the people stopped coming, they had to shut the doors and go away. It is very sad."

"I wish I could come here all the time," said Elise, looking around.

"Me too," said Nia.

"Shall we go for a walk along the beach and see if there are any nice shells and stones?" asked Grandma.

"Sure!" said Elise and Nia.

They started at one end of the beach and walked along the water's edge all the way to the other end, where there was a pile of rocks sticking out into the sea.

They clambered up the rocks and sat at the top.

"Look!" exclaimed Nia. "A boat!" She was pointing excitedly at a large boat, which had appeared on the horizon.

"Where did that boat come from, Grandma?" asked Elise.

"That boat is a yacht. There are lots of sailing boats on the sea around Antigua."

"Are there people inside that boat?" asked Nia.

"Yes, there are," said Grandma. "Can you see the sails? There are people trimming the sails and keeping them in the wind to make the boat move."

Grandma squinted into the sun and then said, "Do you know, once upon a time some little children just like you sat here and looked out to sea and saw a pirate ship!"

"A pirate ship!" exclaimed both Elise and Nia together. "Were there real pirates on the ship, Grandma?"

"Of course, darlings," Grandma said. "Pirate ships used to sail around these islands a lot, looking for other ships to plunder."

"What's plunder, Grandma?" asked Elise.

"Stealing their treasure," replied Grandma. "There weren't any planes in those days, so everything and everyone had to travel by sea. There were lords and ladies and rich merchants, and lots of goods in the holds of the ships. For a long time, there were people in the holds of those ships too."

"People??" asked Elise, opening her eyes and then frowning. "How come?"

"Well, my darling, once upon a time people from

Africa used to be brought here to the Caribbean and sold to the people who owned the plantations."

"You can't sell people, Grandma," said Nia in her know-it-all voice. "That's silly."

"But they did, child," said Grandma. "They sold people and made them slaves, so they had to work on the plantations to grow the sugar cane. The pirates stole from the ships when they tried to get to or from England and Europe."

"Did they sell children too?" asked Elise. Nia was being quiet and thinking about what Grandma had just said.

"Sometimes they did. Aren't we lucky they don't do that here anymore?… But you know," Grandma continued with a sigh, "there are other places in the world where they still buy and sell people and children as slaves. It's a very wicked world."

"I want to go back home to Mummy," said Nia, frowning.

"Yes, let's go home now darlings," said Grandma gently.

They had one last look at the pretty white yacht, which was much closer now, before popping straight back into Grandma's living room.

"Come on girls. Bedtime!" Mummy was just coming through the door. "Be quiet though, Joe's asleep."

The girls gave Grandma a hug before going off to bed. Grandma smiled gently and hugged them back.

"Goodnight, girls," she murmured.

14

THE BEACH AT CHATELAILLON

"Look at that!" shouted Grandma. "See how quickly the tide is rushing in? We have to get up to the beach before we get washed away."

The children held hands and ran, skipping over little pools and scaring the birds, who were having a quick snack on the small fish and sea creatures trapped in the little tidal pools on the shore. The sea had seemed so far away, but suddenly the water was washing in, as though pushed by a giant hand.

The children were in Chatelaillon in France with their grandma and, for once, they had not come to this beach by magic. They had been spending a week with Grandma's friend Maia and her grandchildren by the sea on the French coast. This was the third day. It was Friday. They loved coming with Grandma to visit Maia because she had lots of grandchildren too. They were all the same ages as them, so they were a big group of friends, frolicking on the beach every day.

In the evening when they got back to the little house, they all tumbled into the shower one after the other. They had lovely bowls of soup for dinner, followed by yummy cheese and yogurts for dessert.

It was in fact quite rare that they were all together because Maia's children led very busy lives and never really coordinated things so that they could all be in one place. It was lucky that Maia thought it would be a good idea to have all her grandchildren holiday together without their parents – that made it a lot easier to organise and it was just lucky that Grandma had the same idea!

In the evenings, there were ready-beds everywhere with sleepy little people, tired out after a day of running around on the beach, of running out to where the tide had receded and then running back before it came in again.

They went on an outing to the Ile de Ré and had a great time on the beaches there. They particularly liked watching the kite surfers skimming along the sea at eye-watering speed, with their multi-coloured kites catching the wind, sometimes lifting the surfers high out of the water. There were a lot of birds to watch as well, as they fished in the marshes or swooped into the sea for their prey.

The children talked to one another in their own language, made up of French and English and a lot of hand signals. It was so much fun playing together and making new friends.

One evening as they all sat around eating their dinner

of vegetable soup, grilled fish, cheese and fruit, Nia looked at her grandma and said, "Grandma, I really like it here. Can we come back again another time?"

"I would love it if we could come again," replied Grandma, "but I was thinking we could go and visit Maia in her other house by the lake. We haven't been to a beach by a lake yet, have we?"

"No, we haven't," said Nia. "That would be such fun. Would all the children be there too?"

"We will have to see," replied Grandma. "That would be great, wouldn't it?"

"Yes, they're our friends, and I can speak French now, Grandma! That's what they speak you know," said Elise.

"I know, darling. I'm very proud of you."

"Could Mummy come next time?" asked Nia. "I want to show her when the tide rushes in … and I want to show her the tower on the island."

"Well, we will certainly have to bring her along with us the next time," said Grandma.

Grandma noticed that Coco and Louis were being very quiet. "Are you missing your mummy and daddy too, Coco?"

Coco nodded her head and put her arm around her little brother. Grandma thought for a minute and then said, "I know! Why don't we all Skype your mummies in the morning when we wake up? We can call straight after breakfast."

All the children's faces lit up and they were all happy, thinking about all they would have to tell their parents. Joe and Didi weren't quite sure what was going on, but since all the bigger children were excited and happy, they were happy too. Although they were both now four and five, they did miss their mummies quite a lot. But Grandma had a surprise in store for them…

The children woke up early the next morning and were surprised to find Maia, Papy Bernard and Grandma all awake and in the kitchen making bowls of hot milk and chocolate for breakfast. On the table there were pots of yogurt and *tartines* (chunks of bread with butter) and jars of different homemade jams.

They all were suddenly very, very hungry, and slipped onto the benches, laughing together. Papy Bernard had bought the nutty bread he liked, and there were other different kinds of bread that the children never had at their homes in England. It was all delicious. They also enjoyed eating plain yogurt mixed with fruit or jam.

After breakfast, everybody had to clear away his or her bowl and spoon. Then they brushed their teeth and changed into day clothes. Grandma told her grandchildren (Elise, Coco, Nia, Louis, Didi and Joe) that they were all going out for a walk.

"Are our friends coming too?" asked Coco. She never liked leaving other children out of things.

"Hmmm, I don't know if they want to come along. Why don't we ask them?" suggested Grandma.

"Yes, please!" said Coco with a smile.

Some time later, Grandma with her brood, and Maia with hers (Marc, Lisa, William and Chiara, Théophile, Baptiste and Elliott) started off down the road. They were very well behaved and all held hands and stayed well away from the road, doing as Grandma and Maia told them.

Finally they arrived at the market and went into the bakery to buy bread and lovely fruit tarts. Then they bought cheese and fruit and some fresh fish. The fish seemed to make Grandma and Maia very happy, but the children were much more excited at the prospect of those lovely tarts!

Suddenly Elise squealed with excitement and then Coco and Nia and Louis were all squealing as they recognised some people sitting out on the terrace of the little café. It was their mummies!

They were very excited as they hugged them and all tried to speak at once, to tell them about all they had done with Grandma and Maia. Everyone was smiling and laughing and happy.

That was Grandma's big surprise!

15

THE BEACH AT VERA PLAYA

Head down, pedalling furiously, Elise was enjoying this 'venture specially, because she knew this beach. It was Vera Playa on the east coast of Spain and she had spent a couple of lovely holidays there with her mummy, her little sister Nia, her little brother Joe, and Grandpa and Grandma. Once they had been there with Taty Zou and Taty Lidi and her cousins Coco and Louis and Didi. They had had such fun! But that was a long time ago and they hadn't come for years and years.

Elise was now thirteen and life had changed in so many ways. For one thing they no longer lived in the same house as Grandpa and Grandma. They lived next door!

Elise loved the promenade with the cycle path that went all the way along the coast from Vera Playa to the far end of Garrucha, the little fishing town near to which they had rented a lovely villa.

It was quite unusual for Grandma to go on a 'venture with just one of her grandchildren, but on this day everybody was doing something different. Nia had gone to a birthday party for one of her school friends. Joe was playing football and Mummy had gone to drive him to the match. Mummy had asked Elise if she wanted to come along, but Elise thought she would stay and keep her grandma company. Besides, they almost never got to spend time together, just her and Grandma.

She was glad she had decided to visit Grandma. They were having lots of fun. They had done some writing together – her grandma loved writing stories and she had given Elise her own notebook when she was five so that she could write in it anything she wanted to, a story she made up in her head, or just things she had done. Grandma had explained to her what a diary was and she had been trying to write in her diary every day like her grandma did.

Sometimes she was just too busy on her tablet, dancing, practising gymnastics or doing homework, but most days she managed to write something.

Grandma had said, "You don't have to write for hours and hours because it can be difficult to find that much time every day. But anyone can find five minutes every day."

Grandma was right. It was a lot easier to find five minutes and Grandma had even given her granddaughter a timer, so she could know when the five minutes had passed. Lots of times the timer went off and she kept on writing a bit longer.

Today, Grandma was riding a bicycle too, but Elise was much faster, so she could go ahead and then turn back and ride really fast, back to where Grandma was pootling along.

"Hello Grandma!" Elise grinned at Grandma. "You're so slow!"

"I'm enjoying my ride," said Grandma, "and it looks like you are enjoying your ride too!"

"Yes, I am! But I'm getting really, really thirsty," panted Elise, exaggerating just a little bit.

Grandma smiled. "Why don't we cycle to the *chiringuito* on the beach at the edge of town. We can have something to drink there." Chiringuito is the name for a beach bar in Spain.

"And some ice cream?" asked Elise with her best smile.

"Perhaps we can have some vanilla ice cream there too. Would you like a cone? Or a wafer sandwich? I like those wafer sandwiches with strawberry and vanilla ice cream." Grandma was smiling too.

"Ooh! May I have one of those?" said Elise. Then she changed her mind. "No, no, a cone!"

"Well you certainly could…" said Grandma suggestively.

"Please may I have a cone, Grandma?"

"Of course darling," Grandma smiled, pleased that Elise had asked politely. "Just vanilla then?"

"Oh yes, please!" said Elise with a big smile.

When she was little she was rarely allowed sugary foods because she had an immediate and extreme reaction to sugar. Now that she was much older she was better able to control herself. But it still felt like forbidden fruit whenever she had something sweet.

They cycled the short way to the *chiringuito*, got off their bikes and pushed them along the wooden planks that provided access over the sand to where the beach bar sat only a few feet away from the sea. They found a table near the sea and sat down. When the waitress came to take their order, Grandma asked her in Spanish for the ice creams and two hot chocolates.

Elise was pleased that she could understand most of the conversation. Grandma had always encouraged her grandchildren to learn languages and they all spoke French quite fluently. They spent holidays in France every year and used their Spanish when they went to Spain.

Didi spoke the best Spanish of course, because her daddy and all his family were Spanish. Coco spoke the best French because she had been going to France for holidays with her mummy and daddy ever since she was a baby. Besides, her mummy Taty Zou spoke French quite a lot. Grandma did too. The whole family was French, but it was strange, because Grandpa didn't speak much French at all.

After their ice creams and hot chocolates, they went down to the sea edge and looked out to the horizon. They were near the port and there were a lot of boats moored nearby.

"Have you ever been on a boat, Grandma?" asked Elise.

"Yes I have, darling. When I was a little girl especially, my mummy and daddy used to take me on a really big boat from Trinidad to Martinique. I loved it."

"I wish one day we could go on a boat," said Elise in

a dreamy voice. "But not on a sailing boat! I would be so scared."

"Really?" exclaimed Grandma. "I thought you would love to go sailing. If you learnt how to do it, you wouldn't have to be scared. Often we are scared by things and situations we don't know. The best way to conquer fear is through knowledge. But of course we have to be safe as well. So before doing something we have never done before, we must find out how safe it is..." Grandma stopped and said, "We should go back now, darling, before we are missed."

"Awwww!" groaned Elise. "I don't want this 'venture to end."

"Well, we have to ride back to Vera Playa to return the bicycles. So the 'venture will be lasting a little bit longer," said Grandma with a smile.

"I bet I'll get there before you Grandma!" said Elise and as soon as they got back to the promenade she mounted her bicycle and sped off.

"I bet you will!" Grandma said out loud to no one in particular as she got onto her bicycle and cycled after Elise...

16

THE BEACH AT LE LAC VERT

Nia had just celebrated her fifth birthday and her cousins had been at her house for a sleepover. It was always such fun when they were all together. Grandma made pancakes in the morning as usual and they stuffed their faces with them, trying different toppings. There was no big restriction on food intake for Coco and Louis, so they could eat lots of jam and syrup. Elise had to watch her sugar intake so she got really excited to be able to eat pancakes and jam like Coco!

Nia quite liked her pancakes plain, with just a little butter and maybe some syrup. Coco called it 'makel' syrup.

After breakfast they all cleared away their plates and got ready for a day of playing. The weather was surprisingly mild and sunny, though there was a little breeze teasing the dying leaves and making them dance as they fell from the trees.

Grandma's little apple tree, which grew in a pot on the

patio, had little apples on it and this year Grandma had made sure to cover the tree so that the squirrels could not get at the apples.

The children all wanted to go biking, all except Nia, who had a really full tummy and didn't fancy riding a bike just then when everyone was putting coats and shoes on. She said, "I'm going to stay here with Grandma."

"Come on Nia. Let's go for a ride!" Louis was trying to persuade her to go along. He was very keen to ride his big-boy bike.

"It's OK. I'm too full up. I want to stay here with Grandma," said Nia.

So all the other children – Coco, Louis, Elise, Joe and Didi – all trooped out with their mummies and Uncle Hugo too. Nia went over to Grandma who was washing up after breakfast. "Would you like to read me a story, Grandma?" asked Nia with a cheeky little smile. "Or would you like to play a game of Snap with me?"

Grandma smiled as she rinsed the little frying pan that she had used to make the pancakes. She put it in the drainer and wiped her hands in the towel before saying to Nia, "Of course, darling. Shall we sneakily go off on a little 'venture, just you and me?"

"Oh yes, Grandma!" Nia's eyes were shining with excitement. "A 'venture. A 'venture." She smiled her biggest smile to show how happy and excited she was.

"Are you sure you aren't too full up?" asked Grandma with a grin.

"No, my tummy has digested all the pancakes now!" Nia liked using big words like digested.

Grandma smiled back at Nia and even giggled at what she had said. "You are such a funny bunny, poppet!" laughed Grandma, ruffling Nia's hair a bit.

"You haven't called me poppet in a long time, Grandma. I like it when you call me poppet," said Nia.

"Where shall we go?" Grandma asked, but Nia knew she was really only asking herself, because she always decided which beach they would visit. "I know," said Grandma. "Close your eyes and hold my hand, poppet."

Nia held Grandma's hand and closed her eyes. She heard the 'pop' and then squealed loudly as she felt herself sliding down a hill towards a large lake of still, green water. They stopped slipping and sliding just a few feet away from the water's edge. It was a very sunny day and there were mountains everywhere that Nia looked.

"Where are we, Grandma?" asked Nia as she looked around at the mountains.

"In the Alps," replied Grandma, "at a place called Le Lac Vert. Do you remember what '*vert*' means in French?"

"Yes, I do," said Nia proudly. "It means green. Is this place called the Green Lake, Grandma?"

"Yes, poppet. It's the Green Lake and the water is very cold because we are quite high up in the mountains."

"But where did the water come from, Grandma?" asked Nia, because she couldn't see a river or even a stream anywhere.

"Well, this place is like a bowl, do you see? So when rain falls and the winter snow melts on the mountains around the bowl, it has slowly filled up. The mountain is made of rock, you see, and there's nowhere for the water to go."

"Do you think it's going to fill up and fill up until it overflows one day, Grandma?" asked Nia.

"I don't think so, darling," Grandma answered gently. "Some of the water is surely seeping into little cracks in the rocks and the sun shines so strongly up here, I am sure some of the water evaporates…"

Suddenly they heard a voice and Grandma stopped talking and cocked her head to listen.

A boy came sliding down the side of the mountain, just as they had done.

"*Je cherche un petit agneau!*" he said to them. "*L'avez-vous vu?*"

Nia remembered her French and said to Grandma, "Did he say he's looking for a little lamb, Grandma?"

"He did, poppet. He asked if we had seen it. Shall we help him find it?"

"Oh yes, Grandma," said Nia.

"*Nous allons t'aider à trouver ton agneau, jeune homme,*" Grandma said to the young man. "We will help you to find your little lamb."

They started walking around the lake. "I hope it didn't fall in!" Nia said in a worried voice.

The young man started walking in the opposite direction.

Suddenly, hidden behind a pile of rocks, Nia spotted a splash of white and as they went closer, she could hear a feeble bleating.

Grandma picked up the little creature and cradled it in her arms, telling Nia to go and call the young man over to where they were. Nia shouted in her loudest voice and was startled when her voice came echoing back to her.

The young man could not make out from where the sound had come so Nia climbed up on top of the pile of rocks and waved her arms to attract his attention. He came running.

"*O!*" he exclaimed, "*vous l'avez trouvé!*" He was very happy that they had found the little lamb and he thanked them over and over. "*Merci, merci!*" Then he put the lamb on his back and started scrambling up the mountainside sideways, slipping and sliding a lot, but making his way slowly up to the top.

After a while he disappeared over the top and Grandma turned to Nia and said, "The sun is starting to go down and will disappear very quickly. Sunsets up here in the mountains are very quick. Then it will be quite cold. So I think we should go back home now."

"That was a nice 'venture Grandma. I'm glad we got to help find the little lamb. But I'm hungry so I do want to go home now." She put her hand in Grandma's hand and closed her eyes.

When she opened them again, Grandma was just in time to open the door to let Uncle Hugo, Taty Zou, Mummy and her cousins back in. Taty Lidi came round the back with two bicycles. Everyone was hungry and it got very noisy while Grandma and the mummies made dinner.

"We had such fun on our bikes, Nia," said Elise to Nia. "You should have come along with us."

"I had a good time with Grandma too," said Nia, looking at Grandma who gave her a wink and a smile.

THE BEACH IN THE CAMARGUE

"Quick! Quick!" whispered Coco. "Let's hide in here."
The big children ducked into Grandma's sewing room and
giggled quietly as they heard footsteps along the corridor
outside the room. But it wasn't Didi and Joe who found
them. It was Grandpa! They squealed and tried to escape,
but Grandpa caught Elise and Coco. "No playing in
Grandma's sewing room!" he said before letting them go.

The children were at Grandma and Grandpa's new
house in the south of France. It was summertime and they
were spending a whole month together. There were all
sorts of new things to do, like climbing trees and wading
in the stream. The house was big, with a lovely large room
just for the children. There were bunk beds with enough
space to invite friends or other cousins to visit.

There was a playroom where they could play with toys
or games, and a music room with lots of empty space for

dancing. Taty Zou liked doing yoga there and Grandma used it for her T'ai Chi. There was a TV in there too, but they only ever used it to watch T'ai Chi or yoga or exercise DVDs like Zumba!

The kitchen was really big too, with a large cooker and two really big ovens. Grandma and Grandpa cooked lots of lovely food and the children got to bake cakes and make pies as well. Of course they rather liked going to the village bakery where they could practise their French and buy lovely baguettes, croissants and other delicious pastries.

Going to the village was such fun. The *boulanger* (that's the French word for baker) Monsieur Duchamp and his wife, whom everyone called Madame Jeanne, were lovely and jolly and he was always sneakily giving them '*patisseries*' (pastries) for free.

They would troop in there, all six of them sometimes, or sometimes it would be just the girls, when the boys decided they wanted to go and see Monsieur Laurent on the farm. They were very polite and always said, "*Bonjour Monsieur Duchamp. Bonjour Madame Jeanne.*" Then they would smile when Monsieur Duchamp laughed and said, "*Bonjour Messieurs et Dames*" or just "*Bonjour Mesdemoiselles*" when it was just the girls.

Then he would always ask, "*Et qu'est-ce qu'on vient acheter aujourd'hui? Hein?*" Since he asked them the same question every time, they figured out that it meant, "And what do you want to buy today?" So they would say, "*Une*, or *deux* or even *trois baguettes, s'il vous plaît.*" '*S'il vous plaît*' meant 'please' and they were always very polite.

Then Monsieur Duchamp would ask, "*Est-ce que vous avez de l'argent?*" and he would rub his fingers together, so they guessed that meant 'Do you have any money?' and they would hand over the money they had and Madame Jeanne would count up the coins and tell them "*Merci.*" Then they would say "*Merci. Au revoir.*"

After a while, Madame Jeanne learnt their names and she seemed to like to say all their names. It made them wonder whether she might have been a schoolteacher once, and maybe she missed doing the roll call!

Anyway, that day they had already gone into the village to get bread and had gone to get some lovely ham as well, at the *boucherie* (the butcher's). So at lunchtime, Grandma and Grandpa let them have a picnic with ham and baguette sandwiches, hard-boiled eggs and delicious red tomatoes, which they picked themselves from the vegetable patch. They added apple juice and yogurt and the basket was complete. They spread out a blanket down near the stream and enjoyed their feast.

Grandma liked to have a rest in the early afternoon so they took their time and stayed by the stream, talking and playing silly games. One of their favourite games was pretending they were back in olden days and on their way to find a treasure in a faraway land. They could make lots of noise and not disturb Grandma's nap when they played down by the stream.

Later on they carefully picked up all the rubbish and walked back up to the house. Grandpa was in a lounger relaxing by the pool. "Did you enjoy your picnic then?" he asked the children as they came past him.

"Yes, Grandpa. We ate everything," said Nia. "It was yummy! We love having picnics down by the stream."

"Well, don't be too loud. I think Grandma's still sleeping," said Grandpa.

"OK, Grandpa, we won't," said Coco and Elise together. Then they laughed because they were always saying the same thing at the same time.

"Can we watch the old movies?" Elise asked Grandpa.

"Yes, you know where to find the DVDs," said Grandpa.

The children loved looking at old family movies of when they were babies. The sun was really hot, so they thought they would enjoy being indoors for a while.

They had just finished watching the DVD in the TV room when they heard Grandma calling, "Elise! Coco! Nia! Where are you, children?"

"We're in here, Grandma," called back Coco, "in the TV room."

"Ah, there you are! What have you been up to? Anyone fancy a trip to the beach?"

"Oh yes please, Grandma!" they all said together eagerly.

"Well, where shall we go today, hmmm?" Grandma always asked that same question, but no one ever got to answer, because she always picked which beach they would visit.

"I know," Grandma said as usual. She looked around and said, "Come on then, let's hold hands. You know what to do."

They heard the 'pop' and immediately found themselves on a road in a little village, by what looked like a river. There was a bridge and Grandma led them over the bridge and off to the right. Ahead of them they could see the sun glinting on water.

"Is that the sea?" asked Elise, looking puzzled. "This isn't a real beach, Grandma!" Elise was sometimes a little cheeky and she quickly said, "Sorry Grandma," when she caught Grandma's stern look. They understood each other, the children and Grandma, and whenever one of them slipped into cheekiness, a look from Grandma was all they needed to realise what they had done and apologise.

"This part of France is called the Camargue, and it is very famous. Who can guess what it's famous for?" asked Grandma.

"The river?" guessed Nia.

"The sea!" guessed Louis.

"What is it famous for, Grandma?" asked Coco.

"The horses!" said Grandma to everyone's surprise.

Just then they heard a familiar sound – it was the sound of galloping and a beautiful grey horse went by in a flash.

"Wow!" exclaimed the children as more horses followed and disappeared in the tall reeds, throwing up water from the marshy ground.

"They are all grey!" exclaimed Louis. "I wish I could ride one!"

"Me too!" said the cousins, one after the other. "Me too!"

Then suddenly the horses were coming back and the young man riding one of them stopped close by and held out his hand to Louis.

"Please Grandma, may I?" asked Louis, his eyes shining.

"*Fait attention!*" said Grandma. "Be careful and hold on!"

Louis allowed himself to be hauled up onto the horse and just had time to grab a handful of the horse's mane before it took off at a gallop across the marshes, toward the sea.

All the other children watched in awe and amazement at Louis riding the grey horse. It looked like such fun!

"Please can I try?" asked Elise, jumping up and down a little. She didn't bounce nearly as much as she used to when she was five or six, but she was very excited about wanting to ride that horse. She turned to Coco and asked, "Do you want to try?"

"I don't know, Elise," said Coco. "It's such a big horse!"

"I'm not scared!" said Nia, fixing her gaze on Louis and the horse. They had circled around and were galloping back towards the group.

"I thought you wanted to see my new beach," said Grandma.

"We can all go on the horses, Grandma! Pleeeease!" begged Elise.

"Well I suppose we could if Didi and Joe would like to try it too," said Grandma slowly, looking at Didi and Joe in turn.

"Come on guys, it'll be lots of fun!" wheedled Elise to her little cousin Didi and her own little brother Joe, who were standing very close to their Grandma.

"Do you want to go on a horsie, Joe? Didi?" asked Grandma.

"Horsie!" shouted Joe, suddenly excited as Louis pulled up on the horse.

"Didi ride horsie!" said Didi. "Grandma come too."

A few minutes later, it was an amazing sight to see all of them (Didi rode on Grandma's horse) galloping along the thin strip of sand that separated the still water of the sea from the reeds that rippled in the breeze, under the hot sun of the Camargue.

This was a beach they would never forget.

The First Beach Stories (all but one) took place on these real beaches

#1. The First Beach Adventure – Mayaro on the east (Atlantic) coast of Trinidad

#2. The Special Beach and the Petrified Forest – Sainte-Anne on the south coast of Martinique

#3. The Strange Beach at La Romaine-on-Sea – Gulf of Paria on the west coast of Trinidad [my childhood home]

#4. A Quick 'Venture to the Pink Sand – Accra Beach on the west (Caribbean) coast of Barbados

#5. The Beach with the Hot Black Sand – on the north western coast of Martinique

#6. Blue Waters and Goat Island – on the north eastern coast of Tobago

#7. Meeting Annie and Making Sand Castles – Sans Souci on the north coast of Trinidad

8. The October Birthdays and the Jellyfish Beach – on the shores of the Red Sea, Egypt

9. The Beach in the Wood – Petts Wood in Kent, England

10. Little Bacolet Beach – on the south (Atlantic) coast of Tobago

#11. Gregory – this is the one I imagined!

#12. Back to La Romaine-on-Sea – this was my childhood home in Trinidad (see # 3)

13. The Beach at Half Moon Bay – south eastern coast of Antigua

14. The Beach at Chatelaillon – on the west coast of France

15. The Beach at Vera Playa – on the east coast of Spain (the Costa Blanca)

16. The beach at Le Lac Vert – a beautiful lake in the French Alps, above the Plateau d'Assy

#17. The Beach in the Camargue – the Camargue is a famous region in the South of France